The Private
Notebook of
Katie Roberts,
Age 11

Other novels by Amy Hest:

Getting Rid of Krista
Love You, Soldier
Maybe Next Year
Nannies for Hire
Pajama Party
Where in the World Is the Perfect Family?

Picture books by Amy Hest:

The Crack-of-Dawn Walkers
Nana's Birthday Party
The Purple Coat
Rosie's Fishing Trip

AMY HEST

The Private Notebook of Katie Roberts, age 11

ILLUSTRATED BY SONJA LAMUT

CANDLEWICK PRESS
CAMBRIDGE, MASSACHUSETTS

❀ ❀ ❀

First edition 1995

Library of Congress Cataloging-in-Publication Data

Hest, Amy.
The private notebook of Katie Roberts, age 11/Amy Hest; illustrated by Sonja Lamut.—
1st ed.
Summary: In a series of journal entries and letters to a pen pal,
Katie relates her feelings about her father's death in World War II,
her mother's remarriage, and the family's move from New York City to Texas.
ISBN 1-56402-474-1
[1. Moving, Household—Fiction. 2. Remarriage—Fiction.
3. Diaries—Fiction. 4. Jews—United States—Fiction. 5. Texas—Fiction.]
I. Lamut, Sonja, ill. II. Title.
PZ7.H4375Pr 1995   94-37737
[Fic]—dc20

2 4 6 8 10 9 7 5 3 1

Printed in the United States

Candlewick Press
2067 Massachusetts Avenue
Cambridge, Massachusetts 02140

Dear Kate,
This one's for you.
Love,
me,
Mommy
♡

The war came and took my father forever. I was seven.

Weeks passed. I went to school and the library. Months slid into years. I went to temple with my mother, and bought flowers at the market. Oddly, I could still smile. From time to time, I could even laugh. But always, the question: Why did my father die in the war? Why couldn't he just come home, the way you're supposed to?

More upheaval when I was eleven. That was the year Mama decided to marry Sam Gold. We would pack our bags and our lives and move to Sam's ranch in faraway Texas. My mother danced through the rooms, happy again. But I was scared.

My favorite neighbor, Mrs. Leitstein, came to the station to see us off. She was old like a grandmother, cozy and wise. We held hands in the station but did not talk much. There were pearls wrapped in cotton for Mama, all the more precious because they were Mrs. Leitstein's pearls. And for me, a notebook of my own, beautiful red leather with 100 lined pages. You could use the crispy paper to write letters. Or, you could make it private and write anything you wanted. I did both.

August 7, 1947 5:05 A.M.

Hello Notebook! It's me, Katie Roberts, age 11. From now on, I am going to write down every single thing that happens. Or at least everything important. And remember, this notebook is **PRIVATE!** No one is allowed to see what's inside, and ESPECIALLY NOT MY MOTHER, who is getting married today at noon. (The man she is getting married to is called Sam Gold. I will maybe tell you more about him later, but first I have to talk about me.)

I am sitting on my new bed in my new room in Texas. There's a canopy, which I like. But I miss my old bed in my old room in New York City and . . . I WISH WE NEVER MOVED HERE 8 DAYS AGO. Why? Because I HATE living on a ranch in the middle of nowhere! It is hot here every minute and this house is too big. There are no neighbors nearby. No subways. Not a single tall building. I LIKE CITIES NOT WILDERNESS, AND I AM NO PIONEER!

Mama says new things take getting used to, but she is wrong. Because I will never get used to Texas and I want to go home now.

And one more thing. I don't understand why SHE (my mother) has to get married all of a sudden. We were fine, just the two of us. Perfectly, wonderfully fine. Now everything is spoiled and it's not fair. Well at least I have new shoes for the wedding. Patent leather with a strap across. They look sensational and gorgeous with pink pajamas, which I am wearing right now. Presenting . . . Katie Roberts tap-dancing pajama queen! I like new shoes. And also pink pajamas.

Katie's Shoes (gorgeous!)

More later. After the w_____.

august 7, 6:00 P.M.

Here I am at Mama's wedding. Miss America, HA! My dress has smocking at the waist and tiny rosebuds all over.

I look very pretty.

Mama did not wear a white dress. She wore navy blue. When I get married, I will only wear white and my dress will be a gown. My mother has a new name, which is Mrs.

Sam Gold. She has a new ring, too. It's not that pretty. I like the old one better. My father gave it to her.

We had to drive 30 miles just to find a Texas rabbi, and guess what, he had no beard! I've never seen a rabbi without a beard. This one looked like a regular man and his house was a regular man's house. His wife had red hair, green shoes, and a boy baby called Charlie on her hip. He kept on waving and I waved back. I like babies. When I grow up, I will have a lot. Are you ready for this? THE CEREMONY WAS IN THE KITCHEN! Mama held my hand the whole time and I held hers tight. My stomach was knots. At the end Sam stomped on a glass, which is what you do at a wedding when everyone is Jewish. We all clapped. Even baby Charlie. I was laughing and crying at the same time. Mama, too. Then the groom kissed the bride and she maybe kissed him back. Her hat fell off. I hope that's the end of kissing.

I like weddings and also wedding cake. Especially the kind with whipped cream, and strawberries piled high.

Sam Gold is nice but I wish my father didn't die in the war. I wish he just came home, the way you're supposed to.

Good Cake!

August 14, 4:10 P.M.

Hello again, Notebook! It's me, Katie Roberts, age 11, and I am still in Texas. Mama and Sam the man she married did not go on a honeymoon, but THEY ARE BEHAVING VERY BADLY. They give each other looks and smiles that make me feel left out. I pretend not to notice. I pretend not to care, but I do. For example whenever we drive to town in Sam's old car, they make me sit in back. Dust blows in the window in my mouth and my nose. It isn't fair because THEY sit up front where I can't hear all the things they are saying. Sometimes they sing. The songs they sing are really bad. I like to plug my ears.

Sam took us to the town pool this afternoon. The water is ice! Everyone who goes there knows everyone else. Except me. I don't care, they all look stupid. I swam in the deep end. I went off the high board. There she goes . . . Katie Roberts movie-star champion swimmer! I bet everyone noticed the too-tall girl in a green bathing suit. I bet they are DYING to meet me, ha!

Cows. All you see around here are cows, and also a lot of brownish-greenish grass. Sam used to live in New York like us. But after the war he got this BAD idea to build this dumb old ranch in dumb old Langley. So here I am, stuck for life in the most boring place in the history of the world AND I HATE IT. There is nothing to do in Texas, and no one to do it with, either!

I NEED A BEST FRIEND.

Someone like me with streaky blond hair like my hair sounds nice. We do everything together such as swim at the town pool. We jump in the deep end holding hands and I can teach her how to dive. We laugh all day and tell secrets and lie in the sun on a towel that we share.

I NEED A BEST FRIEND.

NOW!

August 28, 5:02 P.M.

SCHOOL STARTS NEXT MONDAY — **HELP!**
I hope I get sick. Not too sick, just a sore throat or maybe a bad cold. Even in a place like Langley, they can't send a sick girl to school.

The principal sent a letter. WELCOME TO MEADOWLAWN SCHOOL. They make you take a school bus. No one will sit next to me or talk to me, which is all my mother's fault. SHE doesn't care that I am miserable in Texas. SHE doesn't care that I will never have a best friend — or any friend — for the rest of my life. All SHE cares about is her new husband PRINCE CHARMING. And now she is learning to milk cows. Isn't that crazy? She goes around in overalls that are baggy and bunchy like a man's overalls. She forgets about lipstick. She used to look pretty when we lived in the city. She always wore a dress.

MY MOTHER MAKES ME CRAZY MAD!

I am so scared about school. I hope my teacher is pretty. I hope she is nice. No one else will be (nice) to the new girl (me).

September 4, 6:00 A.M.

Mrs. Leitstein wrote me a letter! She wants to be my pen pal! I bet she misses me a lot. Well I miss her, and also her kitchen. Her house always smells good, like cookies in the oven. I wish I could go there tomorrow. We could drink cocoa and talk about things. Mrs. Leitstein is the best person to talk to when you have troubles. She knows exactly what to do. That's because she's old.

September 4, 1947

Dear Mrs. Leitstein,

I do not like Texas. They make you go to school when it still feels like summer. My room has tulip wallpaper. When you look out the window, there is nothing to see. Unless you like looking at a bunch of cows, *Mooooo!*

How are you? Now that we are pen pals, don't forget you have to write back right away please.

Thank you for the notebook that you gave me at the station. I love it! As you can see, I am using a piece of the paper to write you a letter. I write many things in my notebook. All of them are private.

Very truly yours,

Katie

Your pen pal Katie Roberts

September 5, 10:15 P.M.

I turn. I toss. I twist in my bed. Left side. Right
side. Knees up. Knees down. Blanket up. Blanket
down. Pillow puffy. Pillow flat. I lie on my stomach. I lie on my back. I CANNOT FALL ASLEEP!
Why? Because tomorrow is the worst day of my
life. My stomach hurts and my fingers are ice,
but the rest of me is burning hot. Mama says she
was always a nervous wreck, too, the night
before the first day of school. Sam says take it
from him, school is the best place to make
friends. Grown-ups LOVE telling stories about
themselves when YOU'RE the one who is crying
and miserable. They want you to think they
understand about being a child, but they don't
understand anything. Well I hope and pray some
girl, any girl, talks to me tomorrow. She doesn't
even have to be best friend material. And I hope
I'm not the tallest. What if I can't find Room 102
and I'm late and the teacher yells and I die of
embarrassment in front of the whole class? What
if I can't find the bathroom and I
really need to go? And lunch . . . I
can see myself now, ALL ALONE,
me and my egg salad sandwich . . .
I hope Mama puts a nice note in my
lunch bag— that will cheer me up . . .

Good Luck
KATIE.
I sure do
Love You!
Mama

. . . Be right back . . .

I just snuck out of bed. Tried on my first-day-of-school clothes again. Mama made me a skirt with pleats for THE BAD DAY. It is plaid and I love it. New blouse, too. White. My shoes are not new, but I like them anyway. Brown with bouncing tassels.

If only I weren't so skinny. I eat and eat but all I get is tall. My father was tall. Handsome, too.

Here's what I wish. I wish I'd wake up tomorrow in my very own bed in my very own room in New York where there are double-decker buses and Macy's and no smelly cows. My father would be inside asking Mama for two socks that match. He would be shaving and singing. He always sang off-key.

I hope my wish comes true but I know it won't, good night.

September 6, 4:00 P.M.

Guess what? Mr. Keyes my teacher is a
MAN! He is married to Mrs. Keyes
the music teacher. A boy called
Matthew sits behind me in the
classroom. He talks and talks.
I do not like boys.

Mr. Keyes

And I do not like being the new
girl. My skirt is too short and my feet are too
big and I miss my old school where everybody knows me. In this school I have nothing to
say and no one to say it to. It's like my lips are
glued together. Annie and Linda from my class
sat across from me at lunch. Everything they
said sounded like a secret. They were dressed
EXACTLY the same. Same dress. Same socks.
Same hair ribbons. Best friends, of course.

My reading book has a bright green cover
with big gold circles. In science we learned about
plant life in the desert. After that, a girl called
Donna showed me all around the school. I bet
you anything Mr. Keyes made her. Probably he
feels sorry for the new girl. At recess everyone
played around with everyone else. Except me. I
sat on the grass near a tree, pretending to write
in my notebook. I take it everywhere with me.

The school bus was bumpy. I sat alone.

MEADOWLAWN SCHOOL

Here is a picture of Meadowlawn School.
My room is marked with an X. This school is
brand-new. It is too big. A person could get
lost. There's a field out back, and also a pool.
I've never seen a school with a pool!
There's a swim team, too. Matthew told me.

September 10, 5:55 P.M.

My mother and I used to be together all the time
and we used to talk things over. We had no
secrets. Now, every time I want to be with her,
SAM shows up. I am TIRED of his face and I am
TIRED of sharing my mother.

Forget Annie. Forget Linda. Donna, too.
They've got a million friends already, so they
don't need me. Anyway they've all known each
other since first grade and it's not fair. I remember first grade. You have no troubles at all when
you are six. I would like to be little again, and cute.

But there is one girl . . . maybe maybe maybe
. . . a friend for Katie. . . . Well I have my eye on
this girl Lucie in my class. She has long, long,
long blond hair and big black glasses. She wears
overalls to school, and also checkered blouses.
Mrs. Reidy the art teacher made us partners at a
table. Lucie is a very good artist like me. I hope
and pray she'll be my friend.

SUBJECT: GYM CLASS

They make you wear droopy, drippy, bagging
bloomers. UGLY!

SUBJECT: LOCKER ROOM

I HATE changing in front of all those girls. I don't
want anyone to see any part of me, so I change
in a corner facing the wall.

SUBJECT: GOING HOME

I want to go HOME. I want to go there now,
today, right this very minute. I could take a train
all by myself, I know how to do it. No more
Texas! My mother would be sorry, ha!

SUBJECT: MY MOTHER

Sometimes I think my mother likes Sam Gold
more than she loved my father. She's always
laughing when he's in the room. I don't know
what's so funny.

September 27, 8:00 P.M.

My favorite thing in school is when Mr. Keyes reads from his fat book of short stories. I like the ones by Mr. O. Henry. This writer likes to trick you at the end. There's always a surprise. When I grow up, I am going to write stories that trick you at the end. Or I might be a famous swimmer.

It's really disgusting the way Pamela Greer is so popular. She's a show-off and a snob but everybody LOVES her. And guess what she wore all over her lips today? Lipstick! It was a really pale shade of pink, but I know lipstick when I see it. I also know you're not allowed to wear it in school and I hope she gets caught, ha! Of course EVERYONE wants to sit next to Pamela at lunch, but LA QUEEN gets to choose. I wonder if she'll ever choose me?

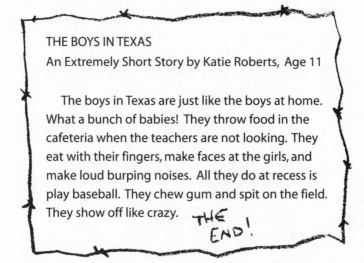

THE BOYS IN TEXAS

An Extremely Short Story by Katie Roberts, Age 11

The boys in Texas are just like the boys at home. What a bunch of babies! They throw food in the cafeteria when the teachers are not looking. They eat with their fingers, make faces at the girls, and make loud burping noises. All they do at recess is play baseball. They chew gum and spit on the field. They show off like crazy. THE END!

Introducing Miss Paulette . . . one day old! Our
new baby calf is the sweetest little baby in the
world! I was supposed to watch her get born but
I was in school when it happened. I am very mad
about that, but Miss Paulette is SO CUTE! Her
ears are flappy like puppy ears. Her eyes are big
and brown. Secret . . . I went to see her in the
barn in my pajamas when no one else was up.
Just me and Paulette all by ourselves at sunrise.
Paulette likes me. I told her I'll come back tomorrow. I told her we'll be secret pals.

Paulette

Paulette pays attention to everything
I say. She likes to hear about city things,
so I talk about the Empire State Building
and taxicabs and bagels. I tell how you
can ride the subway all day long for only
a nickel, on yellow seats that are made of
straw. I tell about surprise April blizzards,
and making snowmen in the park.

I can hear my mother and Sam in the kitchen.
Sam likes to make us pancakes in the morning.
He flips them high up. Sam thinks he's so great.
My mother never ate such great big giant break-
fasts in New York. She had normal things, such
as toast with tea. Now she drinks MILK, on
account of all those cows.

October 14, 1947

Dear Mrs. Leitstein,

   Thank you for your letter. I love when there is something in the mailbox for ME!

   Now I am going to tell you all the news from Texas. First, school: There are 14 girls and 16 boys in my class. Here are the girls: Lucie, Linda, Annie, Judy, Pamela, Wanda, Wendy, Gloria, Thelma, Maggie, Mindy, Deborah, Donna, and me, Katie. (I will tell you the boy names another time maybe). I am good in spelling, reading, and geography. Medium in science. Not good in arithmetic, which is a totally boring subject anyway. I like my teacher Mr. Keyes. I do NOT like the cafeteria. It is too noisy, and everyone sits with a best friend except me. I wish I could go home for lunch, but we live too far. In case you forgot, I had plenty of friends in my school in New York City. In New York I was practically popular.

   I am thinking about sending you a present. When is your birthday, Mrs. Leitstein? How old are you?

   Guess what — Mama milks cows! It is fun to watch but I will never do it myself. Yesterday Mama had tea with a bunch of Langley ladies. She changed her blouse 3 times before they came. The ladies liked her, so now she has friends and a new husband and I have no one. But don't worry, I am fine.

   I made the school swim team! Our bathing suits are royal blue.

   Don't forget to write to your pen pal soon soon soon!

Sincerely yours,   *Katie*

Your faithful pen pal Katie Roberts

my friend
★ LUCIE ★

Well Notebook, here I am again — it's me
Katie Roberts, and something wonderful happened today. What happened is this: I MADE A
FRIEND! It's Lucie from my class, and she likes
me. She asked could she sit with me at lunch,
isn't that the best news in the world! All my
troubles are over. We talked so much, I nearly
forgot to eat. Not Lucie. Boy can she eat! Two
sandwiches, one peach, five chocolate cookies . . .
all that food and she is skinny like a rail. Skinny
like me. Lucie loves to tell jokes. She's got this
little book of them that she hides in her pocket.
Most people think she makes up the jokes, but
now I know the truth. I was scared she would
leave me for her other friends like Thelma and
Deb at recess, but we played catch. To tell you
the truth, Lucie did most of the catching and I
did most of the missing. Then I got a case of the
giggles and Lucie did, too. We just kept laughing,
it was so much fun. After that we watched the
boys on the baseball field. Lucie wanted to play
not watch, but they wouldn't let her. If I were
Lucie, I'd stay far away from boys.

Now hear this . . . Sam is teaching Mama how
to drive! If you ask me, she will never get it right.
There's a dirt road in front of the house where

23

they practice. I like to sit on the fence and watch. This is better than the circus! I can hear my mother in a temper. Sam sounds stern. Sometimes he laughs. Whenever he starts laughing, I do, too. Not Mama. She just gets mad.

Here's a picture ———→

So I guess this has been a pretty good day in Texas.

November 4, 8:00 A.M.

It is Sunday and I am lounging in my pajamas in my room. I love to read under the covers, and I love to write in my notebook. When I grow up, servants will bring me breakfast on a tray every day. Of course I will live in the city, not Texas. I will be a famous writer of important books. My books will be in the library and I will also swim in the Olympics. Miss Paulette will have a room all to herself. She will be the most famous and the most beautiful cow in New York City. We'll take long walks in Riverside Park, and people will snap our picture. Paulette will nibble the grass and city children will pet her, and she will say *Mooooo!*

Mama, the boss of the world, just came by. "Get up, Katie love! Get dressed for Hebrew school!" Well, I don't WANT to get all dressed and I don't WANT to go to boring Hebrew school. Sam drives me over. We have to go a million miles to Temple Emmanuel so I can learn all about being Jewish, even though I already know all about it from my GOOD Hebrew school in New York. Anyway, I get to sit in front, and Sam talks the whole time. He likes to talk about my mother.

All dressed up for temple.

Sam   Me   Mama

November 5, 4:30 P.M.

I am in a VERY BAD MOOD. Why? Because
Lucie who used to be my friend isn't (my friend)
anymore. We had a fight and now I have no one
and I hate this place.

NOSY. That's what she is . . . "Don't you LOVE
Langley, Katie? How come your parents don't
take you to church on Sunday? Don't you LOVE
living in Texas?" Jewish people go to synagogue,
not church, don't you know anything, I said.
Then I said New York is my REAL home and it's
great there. Texas is NOTHING like New York, I
said, and my mother MADE me move here — it
was entirely her idea not mine.

Then I told about Sam's ranch and the cows.
Then — it just slipped out — I said Sam isn't my
father. My father, I said, was a genuine hero who
died in the war. After that, stupid me started to
cry. I ran out of the cafeteria and hid in the girls'
room. So now Lucie thinks I'm just a big baby.
Not that I care. I don't like Lucie anymore. SHE
IS MUCH TOO NOSY. I guess I'll be looking for
a new friend tomorrow. Maybe Maggie.

I HATE THIS PLACE!

November 6, 12:30 P.M.

I am sitting on the grass near a tree in the schoolyard. Alone again. Just me and my notebook at recess. My friendship with Lucie is definitely over. She ate lunch with PAMELA of all people. Well fine! They can be best friends for all I care. Lucie didn't say one single word to me in art. I didn't say anything, either. The picture I made was really bad.

4:30 P.M.

Hello again, Notebook, it's me, Katie-who-has-no-friends. But! I have a job! Sam asked me to paint the fence in front of our house . . . and he is going to pay me some money. You know what I could do with my money? Buy two train tickets, ha! I'm tired of this place. It's not fair that I have to live here just because my mother thinks it's a good idea. We ought to go HOME, just the two of us. Sam can visit. Or, he can stay right here with his cows. If Mama won't come, I'll go alone. Although, a train ride to New York all by myself sounds a little scary.

Anyway, about the fence, Sam says I can choose any color I want, so I am choosing white. Although, I certainly like the color green. Maybe a green fence would be better. Bright kelly green, whoa! Monday after school we are driving to town to buy paint and paintbrushes. I can't wait to get started.

The one and only Katie Roberts GIRL PAINTER

7:15 P.M.

. . . . Guess what! Lucie called! She told me a joke. Then she said, "I am sorry I made you cry yesterday." After that she sighed this great big sigh into the telephone and said she hopes her father never dies. I said I hope so, too.

November 7, 5:55 P.M.

School was a whole lot better today. Why? Because Lucie and I are friends again! We passed notes under the table in art and didn't get caught, whew! We swapped lunches. (I hope Pamela saw that, ha!) Lucie's mom makes great bologna sandwiches. Good news: I got 100% on a spelling test. (Lucie got 96). Not-so-good news: 72 in arithmetic. Mr. Keyes says come in for extra help, but I don't need extra help. I am very mad about that grade. It isn't fair he gave me such a bad grade. (Lucie got 90.) I wish I got 91, and that's all I have to say about boring old arithmetic.

Here we are, two good friends, Katie and Lucie at recess. We are watching the boys play baseball. It is always our class against Mrs. Melby's, and ours is always the big loser. Day after day . . . Strike one! Strike two! Three strikes you're out . . . Lucie calls them PITIFUL. If they'd let HER play, she says, our class would win for a change.

Lucie likes Mindy and Thelma. They take the same school bus, and sometimes they go to each other's houses. I wish someone would invite me.

The swim team practiced after school. Maggie from my class was there, too. You can tell she feels funny in a bathing suit. You can tell from the way she holds her arms. Folded — like a big X across the front of her.

brrr brrr brrr

But boy is she fast! I was hoping I would be the fastest swimmer on the team. If I were, then everyone would like me. Miss Mack makes us swim a million laps, and the water is VERY cold, and you have to wear a tight white cap, and you shiver like crazy when you get out. I love it! Maggie says she's going to swim in the Olympics when she grows up. Or she might work in the rodeo.

I have to go . . . Mama's lighting the Sabbath candles. Every Friday night she makes a special dinner. We use the good dishes. She brought them all the way to Texas, and the lacy tablecloth, too. It used to be her mother's. I love Friday night and the smell of chicken roasting in the oven.

Bye for now . . . .

Mr. Keyes chose ME ME ME to be editor of the class newspaper! In other words, I'm the boss, ha!

In honor of Thanksgiving, we made paper turkeys. Mine is purple, and he won't stand up. We're having a play for the parents. I told Mr. Keyes please don't make me be a Pilgrim all dressed up on stage. Put me on stage, I said, and I'll FAINT, or worse. Well Mr. Keyes is such a great teacher that he's letting me paint scenery instead. Lucie, too. But also two boys called Joseph and Bob.

I wish it would get cold. Thanksgiving is supposed to be grim and gray, and you're supposed to wear a coat. I miss the big parade in New York. My father always took me there on the subway. We'd go early in the morning, while they were still setting up, and stay until the very end. I remember hot chocolate and soft pretzels, Mickey Mouse and Santa Claus. I remember my father's muffler. It was blue.

November 24

Dear Mrs. Leitstein,

68 is not too old. Don't worry. My mother is 34. I am 11. I will try to remember to send you a present for your birthday on July 19.

I can picture you in your kitchen. You are making chicken soup. You are baking cookies, and outside there's a snowstorm. The window ledge is snowy white, but your dress is pink, and so is your sweater. You look very pretty.

I wish I could see you again. We had good times. I loved when you came for dinner, you always wore those pearls. Remember Mama's friend, Louise, the time her baby Rosie was born in a blizzard? I'll never forget that day! But now we're here in Texas, Mama is married to Louise's brother Sam, and you are far away. Are you ever lonely, Mrs. Leitstein? Maybe I can come over and cheer you up. I'll take the train. It is a very long ride, but I don't mind. Because there are berths just for sleeping, and a fancy dining car, too.

This house has a front porch with wicker chairs. Sam and Mama sit there drinking lemonade after supper. They talk too much. My mother acts like she's always lived on a ranch instead of in the city. She acts like this is home.

Yours truly,

Katie

Your good friend and pen pal Katie Roberts

PS: Two things about school —
1. I am editor of our class newspaper!
        VERY IMPORTANT JOB
2. My favorite friend is Lucie. She is the best girl baseball player I've ever seen. Although, I haven't seen too many!

December 15, 7:00 P.M.

Tonight is the eighth and last night of Hanukkah. All the candles are lit and glowy. My father used to eat piles of potato pancakes on this holiday. If I close my eyes, I can see him at our little kitchen table, patting his stomach and saying I CAN'T BELIEVE I ATE SO MANY PANCAKES! When I grow up and write books, they will all have happy endings. In my books the father comes home from the war. He just walks in the door one fine day in his handsome army clothes. He sneaks up behind the little girl's mother who is baking cupcakes and taps her on the shoulder. They kiss a big movie kiss. After that the little girl flies into his arms. And they all live happily together for a long, long time. Possibly forever.

In Hebrew school we had a Hanukkah party. There are just six of us in the class, but it was fun. We sang, and there were grab-bag presents. I picked a pair of pencils. Sam drove me home as usual. We talked about being Jewish. Sam did most of the talking. Sam says you can live anywhere and still be who you are. You can even live in Texas.

I wish it would snow. Even one little flake would be nice. I suppose it never snows in Langley — isn't that sad?

December 19, 8:04 P.M.

OH NO, OH NO, OH NO —
MAMA'S GOING TO HAVE A BABY!

Well THEY think this is the greatest news in the world, but I think it's the WORST. Mama's too old and anyway she's got ME to take care of. What about ME? And Sam Gold doesn't know the first thing about babies or children. All he knows about is COWS. My father knew EVERY-

THING about babies and children. Grown-ups
are ridiculous. They think they're so smart, but
they do everything wrong.

 This is how Mama will
look. Her stomach will be
FAT, which it already is on
account of all those pan-
cakes. Well if she wants
to go around looking like
THAT, fine. I don't care.
Not one little bit.

☆ *Mama
pregnant!*

10:15 P.M.

Hello again, Notebook. I cannot fall asleep
because I am thinking. I am thinking and thinking. Why can't certain people leave things alone?
Just when I am beginning to get a tiny bit used to
living here, they go and spoil it. They never care
about MY feelings. They only care about themselves. A baby. Who in the world needs that?
And by the way, why would anyone pay attention
to ME when there's a brand-new baby in the
house? Babies are cute, and I am not. It's not fair.
And I WON'T babysit, no matter how much they
beg. I won't share my room, either, so they better

not ask. This house is big, but it's not big enough for Baby and me. I wonder if it's going to be a boy baby or a girl? It better be a girl.

<u>December 22, 6:00A.M.</u>

I told Paulette she's not going to be the only baby in town but she'll always be MY baby and I will NEVER stop paying attention to her. When I got back from the barn, Mama was in the kitchen in her old striped pajamas. She used to wear them in the city. Sometimes we had breakfast parties on her big bed in the morning in pajamas. Just the two of us — no Sam, no baby. I was remembering those good times, so I wanted to say something kind and sweet, such as GOOD MORNING MAMA, MAY I HELP YOU WASH THE DISHES BECAUSE I LOVE YOU SO MUCH? but another part of me wanted to say something mean, such as HOW COULD YOU DO THIS TO ME? YOU'RE THE WORST MOTHER IN THE WORLD! I wanted to give her a big hug and ask her to read me a story the way she used to, but another part of me wanted to yell WHAT WOULD DADDY SAY? I couldn't decide what to do, so I came straight to my room to write in my notebook. I am so confused.

Today is the last day of school before Christmas vacation. All the girls are getting dressed up for a special assembly. The boys are wearing ties! I feel funny going to a Christmas assembly. Lucie says don't worry, Wendy's Jewish, too, and David. Sam and Mama are always telling me, be proud of your Jewish roots, and I am, but I do not like being different. I want to be like everyone else. So I will sing Christmas carols and eat Santa Claus cookies.

I am making a list of things I like about Texas.

1. LUCIE

2. MISS PAULETTE

3. MR. KEYES (except arithmetic)

4. MISS MACK my swim coach. Miss Mack likes to call me her City Swimmer. She likes to talk about New York because she is planning to go there one day. To be a Broadway star.

5. THE LANGLEY PUBLIC LIBRARY, which looks like someone's old house. My library card is yellow.

<u>December 27, 9:00 A.M.</u>

Flash! LUCIE INVITED ME TO HER HOUSE! I
am so excited! Sam and Mama will drive me over
at noon. I don't know what to wear. I don't know
how to comb my hair. What if her mother makes
something horrible for lunch that I hate? What if
Mindy is there, or Thelma? I bet Lucie's parents
made her invite me because they feel sorry for
the new girl, sorry for a girl who doesn't know
the words to ordinary Christmas songs. Maybe
I'll stay home and help around the ranch today. I
can learn to milk cows. Sam would like that. I
can write all day in my notebook. Or type a story
on Sam's typewriter which I am allowed to use
anytime I want. My story will have a surprise
ending. It will be about a girl swimmer who does
champion swan dives, and every single person in
school wants to be her best friend.

7:30 P.M.　❀ FUN!

Well I went to Lucie's, and guess what — it was
SO MUCH FUN! She has four brothers and
also a big sister Jennie, who is ABSOLUTELY
GORGEOUS. I wish I looked just like her. Lucie
says boys are always falling in love with Jennie. ✿

Lucie's mom has curly blond hair. She is very sweet, and she never lectures Lucie the way my mother lectures me all day long . . . DON'T-POUT-KATIE and IT'S-TIME-YOU-START-THINKING-ABOUT-SOMEONE-BESIDES-YOUR-SELF-KATIE and HOW-ABOUT-A-LITTLE-HELP- AROUND-HERE-SUCH-AS-FOLD-ING-THE-LAUNDRY-KATIE. Lucie's father looks like a genuine cowboy with leather boots, but he may be a doctor, I think. They have a wonderful Christmas tree there. Lucie has a new doll called Beatrice with a beautiful porcelain face. We made a bed from a shoebox and changed Bea's clothes and pushed her all around in a real baby carriage. I felt funny playing with a doll. After all I'm eleven not seven. But who cares about that, because we had a really good time.

And one more thing. Lucie who loves baseball wants me to love it, too. So we got to work. Throw the ball. Catch it . . . catch it . . . oh, no . . . miss! Throw the ball. Catch it . . . catch it . . . oh, no . . . miss! Lucie's brothers tried to help. Jennie, too. I was PITIFUL. Then the littlest brother brought out a bat. He showed me how to swing. And you won't believe this — Katie Roberts WHACKED the ball over a fence! Beginner's luck, I guess.

January 2, 8:15 P.M.

Back to school and back to arithmetic and back to MEAN Mr. Keyes who made me miss recess today just because HE thought I needed to work on word problems. I DO NOT LIKE ARITHMETIC AND ESPECIALLY WORD PROBLEMS!

Terrible news . . . I think I am beginning to develop in certain places. I never thought it would happen to me, and I am mad. I'm only a little girl, you know. Only 11. And now I am looking bumpy and strange. Especially in my bathing suit. I might just quit the swim team if this keeps up, although my team really needs me.

January 20, 7:30 P.M.

Our class newspaper is called *Talk of the Town* and the first edition is EXCELLENT. Thanks to the excellent editor, me!

The editor gets to choose articles. There's only room for 8. My article is on page 1. It is called "City Girl."

Matthew says it isn't fair that I'm the editor AND my article is on page 1. He's mad because I didn't pick his, but why should I? Nobody wants to read his totally BORING baseball story. I told him to write about something else next time, and don't make it boring. Matthew is so rude. He said since I like the city so much, how come I don't go back? So I said I wish I could, because this place is the WORST place in the world.

Boys are such a pain. Especially Matthew.

January 27, 10:05 P.M.

I am all by myself in the house because Sam drove Mama to school for Open House. I am waiting up because I have to hear every single thing Mr. Keyes said about me. I am in my bed with the covers pulled high. I wish they'd get home. I turned on all the lights in the living room and kitchen. I turned on every lamp in Mama's room, the guest room, and mine. If it weren't so dark outside, I would go to the barn to visit Paulette. But I am scared. This house is too big, and there are strange night noises, and I wish my mother would come home NOW.

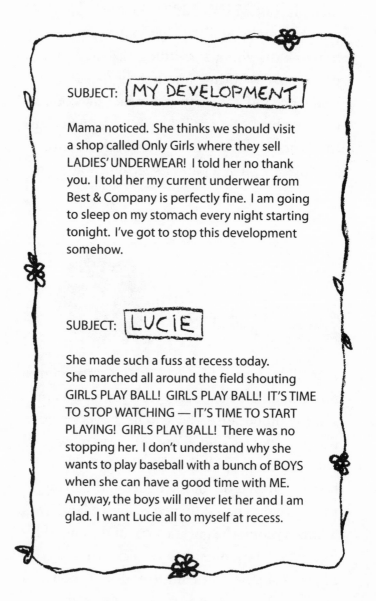

SUBJECT: MY DEVELOPMENT

Mama noticed. She thinks we should visit a shop called Only Girls where they sell LADIES' UNDERWEAR! I told her no thank you. I told her my current underwear from Best & Company is perfectly fine. I am going to sleep on my stomach every night starting tonight. I've got to stop this development somehow.

SUBJECT: LUCIE

She made such a fuss at recess today. She marched all around the field shouting GIRLS PLAY BALL! GIRLS PLAY BALL! IT'S TIME TO STOP WATCHING — IT'S TIME TO START PLAYING! GIRLS PLAY BALL! There was no stopping her. I don't understand why she wants to play baseball with a bunch of BOYS when she can have a good time with ME. Anyway, the boys will never let her and I am glad. I want Lucie all to myself at recess.

10:30 P.M.

I am soooooo tired. They're home and it's about time. Mama came straight to my room. She fluffed my pillow and brushed my hair and said a bunch of things that mean I AM VERY PROUD OF YOU KATIE. I guess Mr. Keyes told her all the right things about all my best subjects. I guess he forgot to talk about math. Good old Mr. Keyes. Good night!

February 10, 5:30 P.M.

I wrote an article called "My Friend Mrs. Leitstein" for *Talk of the Town*. It is a good article. I put it on page 1.

Matthew wrote about BASEBALL again. He is so stubborn. There's this player he loves called Joe DiMaggio. I bet no one cares about Joe DiMaggio except Matthew, but I chose it for page 8, which is the last page. Now Matthew can quit complaining.

February 18, 1948

Dear Mrs. Leitstein,

Thank you for the picture that you sent me of you. I will keep it always!

I am so mad at my teacher Mr. Keyes. He is making a boy in my class called Matthew help me with word problems. So it's me and Matthew the arithmetic wizard every Tuesday, starting tomorrow. Mr. Keyes is the meanest teacher in Texas, and the world.

My mother failed her driver's test. She is very mad! But you know my mother, she never gives up. She is going to practice and practice, then take that test again.

Yesterday my friend Lucie came over. We baked brownies. I showed her the best baby calf, Miss Paulette. We sat in the hay in the barn drawing pictures. I drew one of you.

Sincerely yours,

Katie

Your pen pal Katie Roberts

Mrs. Leitstein ↑

February 19, 9:07 P.M.

Well the arithmetic genius Matthew blabs on
and on about his favorite baseball team, the
Yankees. I don't know why he has to tell me
every single thing about every Yankee in the
world or the Bronx. Matthew mows lawns
around Langley. He is saving up for a trip to
Yankee Stadium. All that work just
to watch a game, and get Joe
DiMaggio's autograph! Anyway I
told him I know how to get there on
the subway. Of course Matthew
doesn't know about underground
trains. So I sketched a little picture.

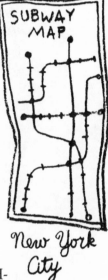

SECRET... Matthew is kind of sort
of cute. Considering he's a boy. Black
hair, freckles across his nose. Blue-
green eyes. Well it's a good thing I
lock up this notebook so no one can
see what's inside. For example, right
this second my face is BRIGHT BLUSH-
ING RED! Isn't that dumb? I don't even LIKE
Matthew. He is the most boring arithmetic tutor
in the state of Texas. He makes me yawn.

February 24, 1948

Dear Mrs. Leitstein,

I have a problem. Sam Gold wants to ADOPT me.
In other words I would be his child. My mother
ALWAYS sides with him, especially now that she is
going to have a baby, and she never sides with me.
She says Sam wants to take care of me as if I were
his own daughter. Well too bad! Because Sam Gold
is NOT my father, and that's all there is to it.

Pen pals should sometimes tell a secret. I will
now tell mine. Sometimes I get so mad at my
father. It's all his fault I am stuck in Texas. It's his
fault about Mama's fat stomach. It's his fault Sam
wants to adopt me and change my name to yucky
Katie Gold. If my father didn't die in that war, then
Mama would still be married to him NOT Sam Gold,
and they wouldn't be fixing up a nursery with
teddy-bear wallpaper. I am very mad at my father,
but I wish I could hug him and kiss his cheek and
smell his after-shave. Isn't that crazy?

Signed,

Katie

Your No–Adopt Pen Pal
Katie Roberts

PS: If you have a secret, you should tell it to me.

February 26, 8:30 P.M.

Tuesday again. Math and Matthew, ha ha ha. We do a little arithmetic, but mostly Matthew talks. Mostly he talks about himself. Today he bragged about his secret trip to Yankee Stadium. He's been saving up for weeks. He keeps his money in a private box that he hides in the back of his closet. If I breathe a word to anyone, he says, I'm in big trouble. I love secrets! So this is the plan according to Matthew.

1. He is going ALL BY HIMSELF, ALONE!

2. But not until April when it is baseball season.

3. His parents love to worry, so there will be a farewell note on his pillow. He already wrote the note, and he keeps it in the closet in the same box with his money.

Well I guess you could say Matthew thinks of everything. If I had money, I'd take a secret trip, too. First stop, New York City! Then Alaska, which we are learning about in geography. In Alaska you go around on a sled. Husky dogs pull you fast through the snow, and you get to sleep in igloos.

I am sorry to say Lucie and I are in a fight, all
because of this crazy story she wrote for _Talk of
the Town_. "Girls Pitch, Too." Lucie thinks
her story is so great. She says it
HAS to go on page 1. I am sick
and tired of talking about BASE-
BALL, I said. Then Lucie said
she's sick and tired of hearing
about NEW YORK — all I ever talk
about is New York. Isn't that nasty?

   And now thanks to Lucie there's a new baseball team — all girls. And guess who made herself
captain — LUCIE, of course. I WON'T be on her
team. And I WON'T put her article on page 1, or
any page. I'm the editor, don't forget. I am BOSS.

   Everything is terrible.

I AM BOSS!
me! me!
me!

March 2, 1948

Dear Mrs. Leitstein,

   I am surprised you are siding with my mother. How can you be so sure Sam loves me? Anyway I don't love him. I like him, that's it. Here's what I like.
   1. Sam tells funny stories and his pancakes aren't bad.
   2. He lights a fire in the fireplace on chilly nights. (I snuggle with Mama on the couch. Whenever I put my hand on her stomach, the baby kicks, which feels very funny!)
   3. Sometimes he reads out loud from one of his millions of books. He wears silly red socks instead of slippers and you can see his toes wriggling inside.
   4. Sam can always get Mama to laugh. Even when she is complaining about being TOO big and TOO tired.
   So as you can see, Sam Gold is very nice. I like him and he likes me, but he is not my family. He is not my father. No adoption!
   Lucie who used to be my best friend is captain of her girls-only baseball team. All of a sudden all the girls in all the 6th grade classes are busy playing baseball. Except me. I'll never waste my recess on a game like that.
   I bet you miss me. You must be very lonely. In case you are wondering, I am old enough to travel on a train by myself. Actually I am quite grown up. Who knows, I might just hop on a train one of these days . . . I might just come for a visit. No one here would miss me.

Signed your old neighbor and favorite pen pal,

Katie

Katie Roberts, age 11

March 5, 6:30 P.M.

My throat hurt in the morning.
Fever, too. No school! It was raining buckets all
day, and gray and cold. I slept, woke up, slept,
woke up. Mama came by with tea and home-
made sugar cookies. She smoothed my sheets
and brushed my hair and felt my forehead and
called Dr. Mason twice. In the afternoon we
looked at old pictures in an album. Just the two
of us, like old times. We cried a little and sometimes we laughed, when we looked at pictures of
my father. Mama misses him like I do. Cinna-
mon toast on a tray for supper. Sam brought a
rose from the garden. It opened right up while I
sipped my tea. You could hear the rain on the
roof. You could see it on the windows.

March 8, 5:00 P.M.

I went back to school today. It felt like the first day
all over again. No friends. No Lucie. I was behind
in reading and science, so I had to stay in at
recess. Which was just as well, since every single

6th grader in this school is baseball-crazy. I could see the fields from the classroom. Girls on one field. Boys on the other. Everyone screaming. Yelling. Cheering. I wanted to go home. I wanted to be with my mother. Mr. Keyes ate lunch at his desk. I pretended to do questions in my science workbook, but I kept on looking out the window. I kept my eye on Lucie. One time she struck out, and I was glad. Which made me feel awful, like the meanest girl on earth, which I probably am. I started to cry. Mr. Keyes was nice. He shared a cupcake from his lunchbox. Chocolate. I told him I have no friends. He said you have to BE a friend to HAVE a friend. Those words keep swirling in my head . . . you have to BE a friend to HAVE a friend . . .

cupcake

So now I have a surprise for Lucie. I am putting "Girls Pitch, Too" in the class newspaper. I am putting it right on page 1. Aren't I nice! Aren't I wonderful! To tell you the truth, it's a very good story. Everyone will read it.

<u>March 9, 12:15 P.M.</u>

I couldn't keep it secret another
SECOND so I wrote Lucie a note during art.
I told her the surprise about "Girls Pitch, Too."
She jumped off the art stool and gave me
a hug and said I'm the BEST friend a person
could ask for and I said I know! Mrs. Reidy
said RETURN TO YOUR SEAT IMMEDIATELY,
and the whole class laughed, but I didn't mind.
Neither did Lucie. We are friends again — we
are friends!

I am sitting way up high on the bleachers.
The rest of the world plays baseball. They shout.
They hoot. They howl and boo and grunt. Even
Pamela, La Queen. Lucie is boss of this field,
though. Right now she is trying to boss me into
playing but I have a case of the giggles, and
anyway I am writing in my notebook. I
promised Lucie I will play. But just a
little, and not every single day.

March 14, 5:30 P.M.

Hello Notebook, guess what! Matthew needs an assistant. Which is why I get to mow lawns around Langley! Of course he gets to do the actual mowing, which everybody knows is the easy, fun part of the job. I do the raking. Not easy, but kind of fun for a city girl like me. Texas grass smells nice and sweet. You can sprinkle it in your hair, just for the heck of it. Matthew says I'm ridiculous. Too bad! By the way, I get 25 cents a lawn. I told Matthew it isn't fair that he gets 50 cents. He said take it or leave it. What a big shot.

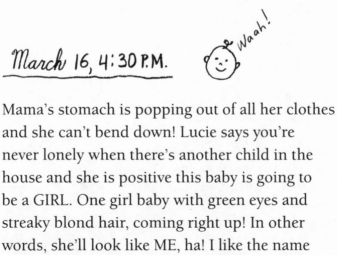

March 16, 4:30 P.M.

Mama's stomach is popping out of all her clothes and she can't bend down! Lucie says you're never lonely when there's another child in the house and she is positive this baby is going to be a GIRL. One girl baby with green eyes and streaky blond hair, coming right up! In other words, she'll look like ME, ha! I like the name Lydia. But her other name will be Gold. Looks like I'll be the only one in this family with the last name Roberts. It's not fair. Unless Sam adopts me. Then . . . Katie Gold ???? . . . Katie Roberts . . .

And one more thing. If Sam adopts me, what do I call him?

Daddy. No!

Dad. No!

Father. No!

Mr. Gold.   Maybe.

Sam.

His name is Sam and that's all there is to it. I am so confused. I have too many problems, it isn't fair.

March 21, 5:00 P.M.

This is a picture of me on my beautiful, new, gorgeous, green bicycle. A present from Mama and Sam, and it isn't even my birthday! I am riding to Matthew's house. His mother makes lemon-ade. Then we go around his neighborhood mowing and raking the lawns. What a team!

Here's Sam, showing me how to milk a cow. *Squirt, squirt!* City Girl Milks Cows! Sometimes I miss New York, I tell Sam. He looks sad, so I say, other times I nearly like it here. Now Sam smiles. Then I ask, how come you married my mother? Sam says these exact words: I love her, Katie, and I love you, too.

That's me . . .
running out of the barn.
I run very fast.

March 28, 10:30 P.M.

I'M IN TROUBLE WITH THE LAW!
(my mother)

Here's what happened. Lucie came over after school. We made covers for our book reports, which was fun. Then she brushed my hair into a French twist so I'd look grown up, like her sister Jennie. I tried doing hers. Too much hair. Then Lucie got this great idea. LET'S CUT MY HAIR! I WANT IT SHORT, CUT AWAY! So I did. We had so much fun, laughing like laughing hyenas — and all that long blond hair on my bedroom floor. Katie Roberts, Expert Barber! Does Lucie like her haircut? You better believe it. She loves that you can see her ears. And doesn't mind a bit about the crooked piece in back.

Now the bad part of this story. Lucie's mom had a fit. She even called Mama. So now I am punished, all because of a silly haircut that makes Lucie look a thousand times cuter anyway. I am banished to my room every day after school for a week, and also next weekend. No bicycle. No raking. No drives to town. No trips to Lucie's house, and she can't come here. It isn't fair.

April 4, 1948

Dear Mrs. Leitstein,

   I am punished. All I did was give my friend
Lucie a sweet little haircut. I know it's not the best
haircut in the world, but Lucie likes it fine. Grown-
ups get grumpy about the silliest things. They act
like they are perfect, but they're not.
   By the way, I'm a working girl now. My job is
mowing lawns. Actually a boy called Matthew
gets to mow. I rake it all up and put the grass in
baskets. I make a quarter a lawn. I guess you
could say Matthew is my friend. Even though he's
a boy.
   I miss you so much, Mrs. Leitstein. You are the
only grown-up who understands me. But don't
worry about me, I am fine.

Yours truly,

Katie

Your pen pal in jail in her room, Katie Roberts

This is what I look like at the swim meet. I am the skinny one in Lane #3.

Swim, Katie, Swim!
Pull! Pull!
Touch the wall and flip . . .
Pull! Pull!
Elbows up!
Reach! Reach!
Go, Katie, go!

Well, Meadowlawn is the big winner this time. Sorry, Barnum Woods School. But we've got Katie Roberts on our team, La Champion!

After the meet, Sam and Mama take me to Flora's Ice Cream Shoppe on Main Street. We all have ice cream sodas.

58

<u>*April 14, 4:00 P.M.*</u>

TOP SECRET INFORMATION . . . . Matthew's
Aunt Gloria must be a millionaire. Because she
sent him ten dollars for his birthday. Sooooo
now he has enough money for his ticket to
Yankee Stadium! He even has extra. Matthew
really is excited. Imagine going on a train all
alone, and all the way to New York. I made
him a map. Aren't I terrific! This is where
you get off the train at Pennsylvania
Station. This is where you get the subway that will take you to Joe DiMaggio.
And this is where my friend Mrs. Leitstein
lives. Just knock on her door — she will cook
up a storm for supper. She makes wonderful
chicken soup, and she will tell you many stories.
Good ones, not the boring kind that parents tell.
And she will NEVER lecture. Matthew likes my
map. He folded it up and put it in his pocket for
safekeeping. I bet you anything he's scared.

But he wouldn't be (scared) if I went along.
Think of it! I could surprise Mrs. Leitstein. I'd
visit the library and the temple, and also my
school where all the girls would hug me. I could
swing on the swings in Riverside Park and watch
the Hudson River.

April 15, 1948

Dear Mrs. Leitstein,

Remember the boy Matthew I told you about?
Well guess what — he is coming to New York to
meet a famous man, Mr. Joe DiMaggio. The train
he is taking leaves Langley next Friday. Don't be
too surprised if Matthew rings your bell, because
I told him all about you. His hair is black and his
eyes are bluish-greenish, and he isn't bad to look
at. But beware, he will talk all day long about the
Yankees and baseball!

   By the way, two other girls in my class —
Pamela and Maggie — asked if I could cut their
hair like Lucie. I told them I'm not in the barber
business anymore, ha!

Your friend,

Katie

Katie Roberts

PS: Passover is coming. I wish I could come to
your house for the seder. Wouldn't that be fun!
We could light candles and eat matzo ball soup.
You wouldn't be lonely.

April 17, 9:30 P.M.

Hello Notebook, this is Katie Roberts, the most unloved girl in Texas and the world. Why? Because my own mother doesn't love me. She only loves SAM. And also that HATEFUL baby in her HUGE and HATEFUL stomach. Now I know the truth.

Here's what happened . . . Sam has been building this baby crib, a surprise for Mama. Every night after supper, he sneaks out to the toolshed to work on it. Tonight he finished. The crib is painted yellow. There are painted ducks, too, and wheels on the bottom so you can push it around. (I will never say it to Sam or my mother, but the crib he made is the most darling thing in the world.) Mama was out front hang-ing laundry on the line, so Sam and I carried it up the back steps. We rolled it right into the nursery, which is right next door to MY room of all places.

When Mama saw the crib, she started to cry. She cried and cried! Sam looked sad, like maybe he painted the ducks the wrong color. Finally my mother said . . . and I quote . . . I've never been so HAPPY in my whole life. . . . She said it only to SAM, and she patted her stomach, and she never once looked at ME. It was like I wasn't even in the room or the house or anywhere.

So now I know the truth about my mother. She loves Sam more than me. And she already loves that baby more than me, too.

I wish I could run away from this place and never come back. They can take their crib and their baby and have a great time without me. I wish I were six. Everything was wonderful when I was six.

I am going to bed and I WON'T say good night to them. I'll pretend I am sleeping when Mama comes in to kiss me. She always does that, and whispers, Sweet dreams, Katie. I don't know why she bothers — she doesn't even mean it. I'm just an obligation. Well fine! She can save up all her kisses for BABY. See if I care!

April 18, 5:45 A.M.

I've made my decision once and for all. I am going with Matthew. To New York. I can't wait to tell him. My mother will be sorry.

5:00 P.M.

Flash! Flash! Matthew says it's OK — I can go!
He says I'm always talking about going there
anyway, so this is my big chance. But I have to
follow his rules and I have to keep it secret. Not
a word to my mother. Or Lucie. My ticket costs a
lot, so Matthew is giving me some of his birthday money. Well, isn't he nice!

I am so excited! Good-bye Texas, ha! I am
going home! That Matthew is some good pal.
This is the greatest day of my life. I have many
things to do:

1. WRITE TO MRS. LEITSTEIN
   (or should I be a surprise?)

2. PACK RED VALISE, HIDE VALISE IN CLOSET
   pajamas
   plaid skirt
   toothbrush
   hairbrush
   bathing suit
   sandwich/cookies
   warm sweater, underwear, socks
   notebook!!!

3. WRITE A FAREWELL NOTE TO MAMA (and Sam?)

4. TELL LUCIE THE PLAN
   (I promised Matthew to keep it totally secret, but I've
   got to tell someone . . . and after all, Lucie is my best
   friend . . . but she better not tell a soul and especially
   not her mother.)

April 19, 4:30 P.M.

I told Lucie. I AM GOING TO NEW YORK WITH MATTHEW, I said, AND THIS IS ABSOLUTELY SECRET. She started to cry. Lucie thinks I'm never coming back. She sniffled all through geography, then spelling. Mr. Keyes sent her to the nurse, but of course she didn't have a fever. We sat on the bleachers at recess. Lucie says if I promise to come back to Langley, she promises not to make me play baseball. I told her baseball isn't too bad, if you're in the mood. I found this note in my desk.

> Roses are red
> violets are blue
> when you go away
> I'll be thinking of
> you
> Love,
> Lucie

I wrote one back.

> Roses are handsome
> Violets are pretty
> You're my best friend
> In Texas and New York City
> Love,
> Katie

April 19, 1948

Dear Mrs. Leitstein,

Get ready for a wonderful surprise!

Signed,

Katie

Your pen pal Katie Roberts, world traveler

April 22, 11:30 P.M.

I am SO NERVOUS! Tomorrow is THE BIG DAY.
Mama will be sorry, but it's too late now. I
washed all the dishes tonight. Dried them, too,
and put them away. I folded my blouses and
made perfect piles in the drawer. I ironed every
single thing in the ironing basket. Mama sure
will miss all the millions of chores I do around
this house. She will miss me when I'm gone.

Today she was getting ready for Passover. Our
first Texas Passover. I can't imagine this holiday

without her. Well too bad. Because I am going home. Next Friday night I can visit our old temple. Everyone there will be happy I'm back. They will say I look more like my father every day. I will tell them about Texas.

CHECKLIST
✓ VALISE PACKED
✓ BICYCLE READY
✓ SANDWICH
✓ FAREWELL NOTE

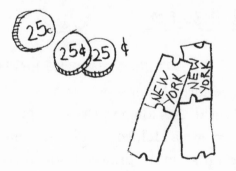

Dear Mama (and Sam),

I am going away, but don't worry. I have a chicken
sandwich and my toothbrush. I remembered a
warm sweater. Happy Passover.

   I wasn't planning to tell you where I am going,
but I changed my mind. I am going home. To New
York. I know you think Texas is perfect. It's not
terrible here. I like the ranch, Miss Paulette, and
school most days. I am glad Mama finally passed
her driving test. I will think of you often. The train
leaves Langley at 6:00 A.M. I will ride my
bicycle to the station. In New York I
will live with Mrs. Leitstein. She is
lonely and old. I can help her with things.
She misses me.

   Well I hope you and the baby are all
very happy together, which I know you
will be now that I'm not in the way. I will
write when I get settled. By the way,
Matthew from my class is coming along.
He has an appointment with Mr. Joe
DiMaggio.

Sincerely yours,

Katie

Katie Roberts

April 23, 6:00 A.M

Guess what, I am on the train to New York! My fingers are shaking, and my hands. I might get sick to my stomach but who cares, because here I am sitting next to Matthew and we are going to New York, ha! The whole time I was riding my bicycle to the station on the dark road, I was CRAZY-SCARED. But Matthew met me like we planned and we hid our bikes in the bushes. The train is long and silver. When the whistle blew, all of me shivered. We told the conductor we were going to our uncle's funeral. We pretended to cry.

6:30 A.M.

First stop after Langley will be Little Creek Falls. I am so excited. And SO SCARED — I don't know why. I wonder if Mama read the note? I wonder if she cried? I miss her. Isn't that crazy? I've never been away from my mother before. Not overnight. Well too bad! She should have paid more attention to me.

6:40 A.M.

Matthew does not understand that I need quiet when I am writing in my notebook. He keeps talking. And punching his fist into the baseball mitt DiMaggio's going to sign. How can I think with all this noise? What I am thinking about is living with Mrs. Leitstein for my whole entire life. I couldn't do that. A year sounds good, or maybe one week. It wouldn't be fair to Mama. Sam might miss me, too. He's the one who wants to adopt me, right? And take care of me like an official daughter, right?

7:20 A.M.

Well, Matthew forgot his sandwich. I had to share mine, and he was mad because he likes scrambled eggs for breakfast, not chicken. Too bad. I have some money in my pocket. I hope there's enough for a glass of milk in the dining car, and also the subway ride to Mrs. Leitstein's. I hope she is home when we get to the City. I wonder if Mama is worried. You're not supposed to worry when you are going to have a baby. I am trying not to cry. Matthew mustn't see me cry. He will think I'm a coward. Which I am. More later . . .

<u>April 23, 8:20 P.M.</u>

Hello Notebook, it's me Katie Roberts, age 11, and I have so much to tell you! You can't believe all the things that happened today. WE GOT CAUGHT. Guess who was waiting at the station when the train pulled into Little Creek Falls? Sam. I was mad and glad at the same time, but I only acted mad. Sam grabbed my valise and Matthew's suitcase and we followed him off the train. I felt like a criminal! Sam never said a word, except HURRY. Then he pointed to his old black car, which was parked at the station. Mama was in the front seat. I wanted to jump in her lap and hug her and tell her I was sorry. But I didn't do any of those things. Because THEY had spoiled my running away to New York. Then guess where we went? STRAIGHT TO THE HOSPITAL BECAUSE MAMA WAS GETTING READY TO HAVE THE BABY THREE WEEKS EARLY!

The minute we got there, they took her away. I didn't like that. Sam and Matthew and I went to a waiting room to WAIT. I wanted to say something nice to Sam but I couldn't think what. Matthew's parents came. His mother hugged him so hard, I thought he might break. Then she bawled him out like crazy and they went home. I wanted MY mother. What was taking so long? It shouldn't take so long just to have a baby. What if something was wrong? Mama could die. I started to cry. Sam held my hand. I didn't let go.

A long time later a nurse came by. Sam stood up. The nurse whispered in his ear. Sam sat down. Then he laughed. He laughed and laughed. TWINS! TWIN BOYS!

I HAVE TWIN BABY BROTHERS! They are the best little babies in the nursery or anywhere else in the universe for that matter. Their names are Billy and Seymour, and they are coming home with Mama in five days.

I CAN'T WAIT!

And one more thing. Mama and I made up. I love her so much and she loves me so much. I cried buckets when I finally got to see her. I just couldn't stop. Then we talked about everything. I told her she never pays attention to ME anymore and she only pays attention to SAM and they make me feel left out and I'm too tall and not cute at all. Then it was Mama's turn. She said I mope and pout and spend too much time feeling sorry for myself. She said I could try a little harder with Sam, for example. Then . . . Lecture #2000 . . . grown-ups have feelings, too, and you can't go through life pushing people away, people who love you. Then she promised to pay a lot of attention to me if I pay a lot of attention to Billy and Seymour.

April 24, 5:21 A.M.

I've been thinking about all the people in this house with one name and me with another. And I've been thinking about my father. What would he say? Adopt or no adopt? I bet he would like Sam. After all, Sam is watching out for us, right? Maybe my father would be happy Sam wants to take good care of me, since he can't be here to do it himself . . .

Katie's **NO ADOPT** *List*

1. Sam is NOT my father.
2. I need MY name because it is my father's name.
3. Katie Gold is a name that has nothing to do with me. Katie Roberts, Katie Roberts, THAT'S me!

Katie's <u>ADOPT</u> List

1. I like Sam.
2. Sam loves me!
3. I kind of sort of love Sam, maybe, <u>just a little.</u>
+ 4. Billy and Seymour
5. Mama

─────────────────────

=   One family

April 24, 8:10 P.M.

Sam and I ate sandwiches on the front porch for supper. There was a nice breeze. I told Sam he could adopt me if he still wants to, which he does. I told him I want to keep my own name, though, just the way it is. KATIE ROBERTS IS A BEAUTIFUL NAME. That's what Sam said. He kissed the top of my head.

Four long days until my mother and the babies are back on the ranch. How in the world can I possibly wait?

April 28, 1948

Dear Mrs. Leitstein,

Sam told me you called long-distance because
you had a sneaky suspicion I was on my way to New
York. I am sorry my visit did not work out, but it's a
good thing I am here in Texas right now because . . .
are you ready for this . . . we have twins! I was hoping for a girl, but Seymour and Billy are so incredibly
wonderful. I love them to pieces even if they are
boys. They came home from the hospital today.
This house is crazy-wild!

Anyway, I am very good with babies, and they
need me around here, so I won't be able to come to
New York too soon. (Matthew isn't coming either,
due to the fact that his parents won't let him go
anywhere but school for the next six weeks.)

I am thinking two things.
1. I wish my father could see the babies. I know
he can't, but I bet he would sing them a silly
song.
2. I was wondering, how would you like to visit us
HERE in Texas?!! I know this place takes getting
used to, but really, it's not so bad. You could stay
a week or a year — as long as you like. You can
meet Lucie and Miss Paulette. I will show you my
school and the library and a funny street called
Main Street, which is nothing like Broadway.
Please say yes! Just take the train from
Pennsylvania Station and we will meet you at the

station in Langley. We'll all be there . . . Sam and
Mama, Seymour and Billy. And I will be there,
too, with the biggest hug you can imagine.
Please say yes!

Love and kisses,

Katie Roberts

Me, Katie Roberts, age 11

Love and kisses xoxo